MW00948414

Yellow Boatie

On Blue Hill Bay

Yellow Boatie

On Blue Hill Bay

Helen Sylvester

Illustrated
by Chris Gray

Published by
WoodenBoat Books
Naskeag Road, PO Box 78
Brooklin, Maine 04616 USA
www.woodenboatbooks.com

ISBN 10: 0-937822-97-3
ISBN 13: 978-0-937822-97-5

First Printing 2008

Book design: Grace Bell

Printed in U.S.A. by Taylor Publishing

10 9 8 7 6 5 4 3 2 1

This Book Belongs to:

____

Yellow Boatie was always a happy little boat, but today he was *very happy*. This was the day he would leave the safe, snug barn where he had spent the winter, to go out on the water of beautiful Blue Hill Bay in Maine.

Yellow Boatie's owner, John, fished for lobsters and crabs in the bay. John's big lobsterboat, *Magic Carpet*, was moored there.

It was Yellow Boatie's job to take John from the shore, out to the big lobsterboat in the early morning. He was proud of his job and was always careful to do it just right.

When the sun would come up over nearby Long Island, the red and gold of the sky would always make him feel good.

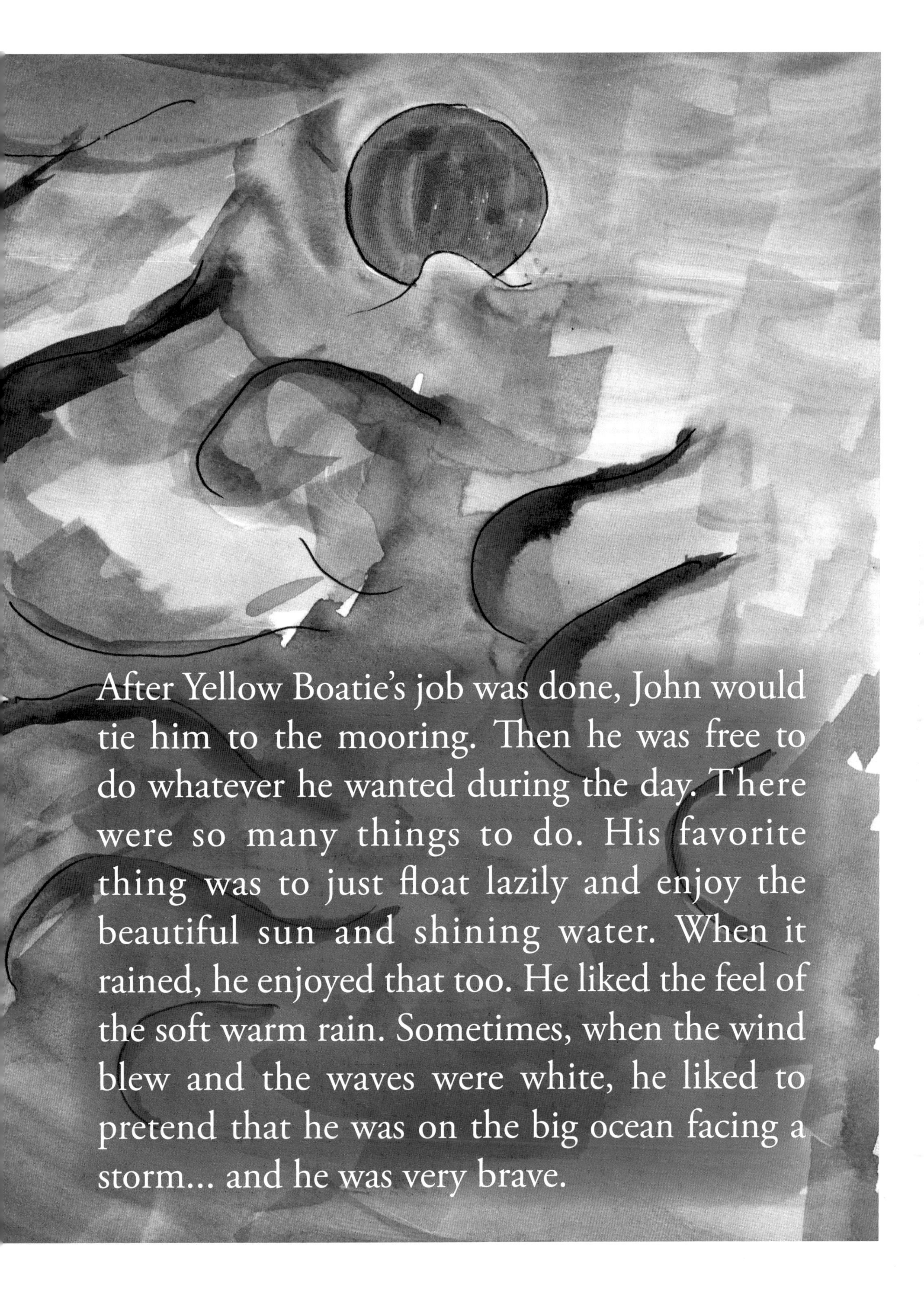

After Yellow Boatie's job was done, John would tie him to the mooring. Then he was free to do whatever he wanted during the day. There were so many things to do. His favorite thing was to just float lazily and enjoy the beautiful sun and shining water. When it rained, he enjoyed that too. He liked the feel of the soft warm rain. Sometimes, when the wind blew and the waves were white, he liked to pretend that he was on the big ocean facing a storm... and he was very brave.

Most of the time, the water was calm and some of his friends would come by. He liked the seals with their shiny gray skins.

Bobbing out of the water, they would play with him. Little Sami was the baby, and Yellow Boatie watched out for him, even though Little Sami's mother was always nearby.

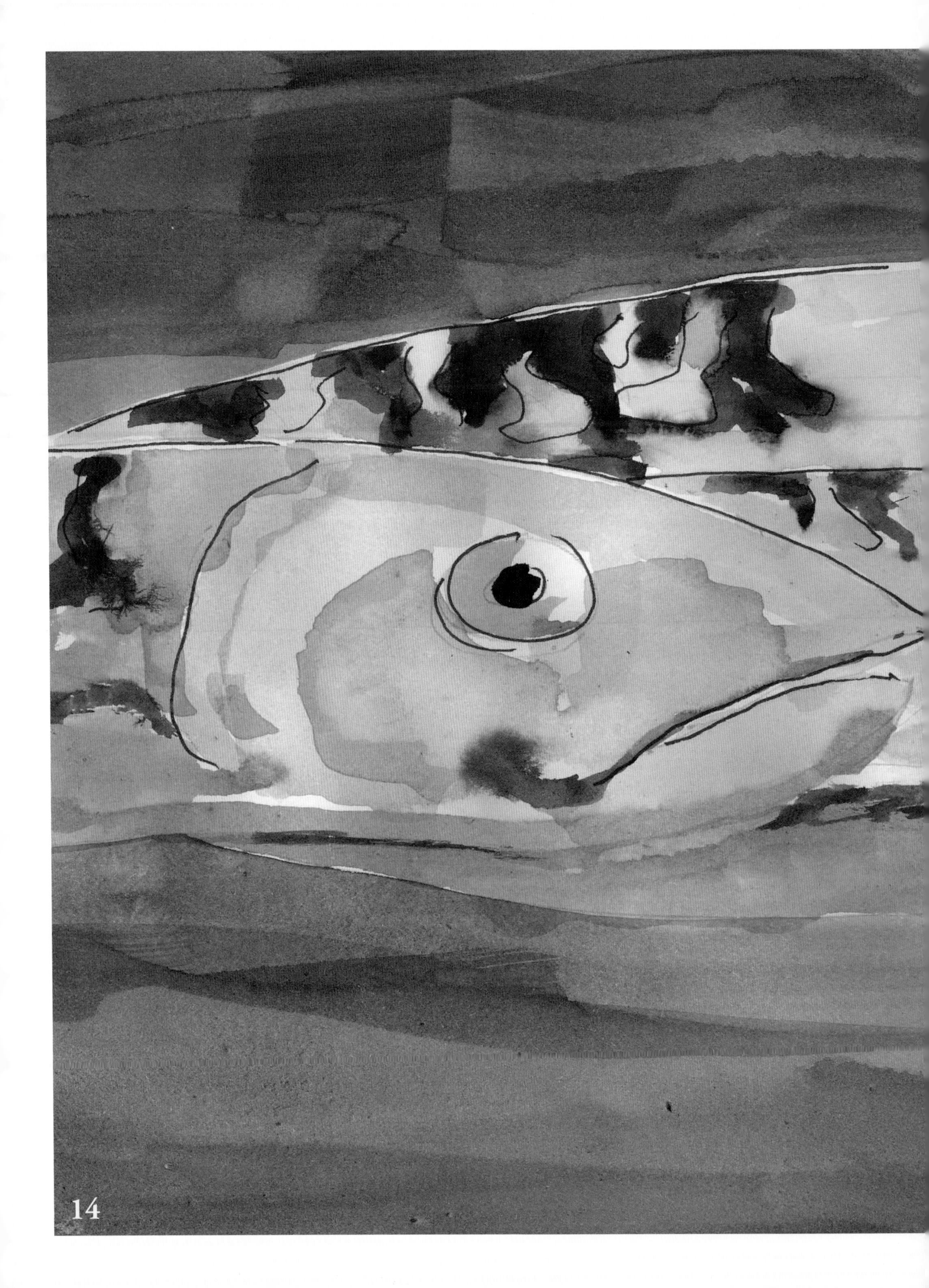

When summer arrived, so would the mackies. Big schools of silver-blue mackerel fish would swim into the bay, and the seals would chase them.

Sometimes black and white loons would float on the water close to Yellow Boatie. What grand birds! They had a strange wild call that sounded like laughing.

And then there were the seagulls, led by Gulliver Gull. Yellow Boatie enjoyed having them perch on the dock pilings and tell him of their adventures.

The gray and white gulls flew over the bay and across Long Island. In the summer, the wind was warm and usually blew gently. The gulls soared gracefully on the wind, providing hours of entertainment for Yellow Boatie.

When lobstermen would pull their traps from the water, a flock of noisy seagulls was sure to follow. The seagulls knew that after the fishermen had taken the crabs and lobsters from a trap, the old bait would be thrown into the water. The gulls swirled, screamed, and dipped, to be sure they got their pieces of fish.

Other times, Yellow Boatie watched as a seagull would take a clam or mussel in his beak, fly into the sky, and drop the shellfish on the rocks or ledges below. The shell would break open, making it easy for the gull to get to the sweet food inside.

After the excitement quieted down, he liked to drift out as far as his long rope would let him, and then drift gently back. Sometimes, on warm sunny days, the children would come down to the shore with their mother. Yellow Boatie liked to hear them laugh as they swam and splashed in the clear cool water.

Every summer there were exciting adventures, but this summer had been the best of all.

At the end of one day, when John returned from fishing and Yellow Boatie had taken him to shore, something happened. Frank, another fisherman, returned to his mooring only to find *his* little boat was gone! The wind had been blowing hard all day long, and Frank's little boat had untied itself and drifted away. Frank could not get back to shore.

John saw that his friend needed help. He jumped into Yellow Boatie, and rowing quickly, they picked-up Frank. Down the bay the three went, trying to spot Frank's little boat. They saw it sitting safely on Long Island, so they rowed Frank onto the beach. When John and Yellow Boatie got back to their shore, John patted him on the bow and said "A good job well done, Yellow Boatie. You're the hero of the day."

By the end of summer, the warm days turned cooler. Yellow Boatie noticed the leaves on a nearby maple tree were changing color—from green, to yellow and red. He knew that soon John would come to take him back to his safe, cozy barn to spend the winter.

He was almost as happy at the barn as he was on the bay, because he was back with his friends.

Yellow Boatie's best friends included: Ma Ma Mouse, Pa Pa Mouse, and the mouse children—Wee Mee, Cee Cee, and Tee Nee.

And there was Haylee, the barn cat, who got her name because she liked to sleep in the hay. They were a very special group of creatures because they looked out for each other. Usually cats and mice do not get along, but Haylee never bothered the mice. She even let them climb on her back and play with her tail. The mice squealed with joy, and Yellow Boatie always liked their play.

Yellow Boatie was not the only boat stored in the barn. Another boat was there, a sixteen-foot long dory named Dorgan. He was Yellow Boatie's hero. Years ago he was used for fishing down on the big bay. Two men with oars rowed the big boat. When they got to a good spot, they put fishing lines with big hooks over the side of the boat and into the water.

They caught cod, flounder, cunner and halibut. What stories old Dorgan could tell! He had been one of the most powerful boats around, and he still had an important look about him.

DORGAN
DORGAN

Yellow Boatie watched over the cat and mice, but old Dorgan watched over Yellow Boatie. Dorgan didn't go out on the water much anymore. He had worked hard for many years, and now it was time for him to rest. He was such a handsome old boat, that lots of people stopped by the barn just to see him.

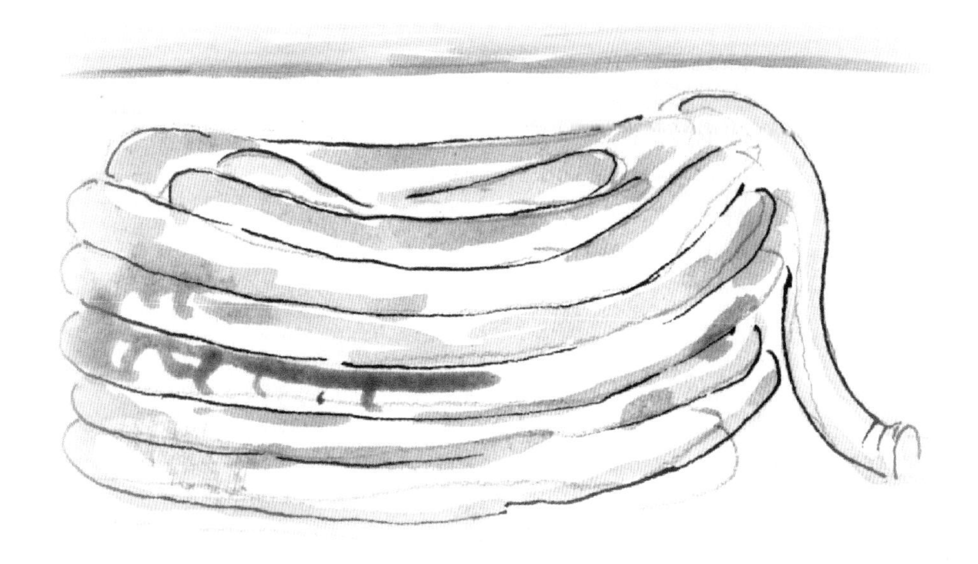

Soon it was winter and the snowflakes fell softly and silently to the ground, covering everything in white. In the middle of winter, excitement started to grow in the barn. It would be Christmas soon, and that was special for Yellow Boatie and his friends.

On Christmas Eve, the nice people who owned the barn would come in very softly while Yellow Boatie and his friends were asleep. They would bring a little Christmas tree decorated with strings of popcorn and little silver balls, and of course there were presents. Haylee's gift was "catnip"—leaves that cats like to roll in. For the mice, there were little pieces of tasty cheese, and Dorgan got a new coil of rope to tie on his bow.

And what do you think Yellow Boatie got for Christmas? Under the little tree was a shiny silver can tied with a big red bow. It was sunshine-yellow paint—which was very exciting because Yellow Boatie just *knew* John would soon stop by with a paintbrush to give him a new coat. He liked the strokes of the brush as John put on the paint, and he knew how good he would look and feel on the bay next summer.

For Yellow Boatie and his friends, the winter would go by quickly. And then one day, as if by magic, it turned warm outside. The birds that had gone way down south for the winter, had come back to Maine. They were singing because their long trip was over, and they were so glad to be in this beautiful place. The robin, Yellow Boatie's favorite, was singing, too. Spring had arrived.

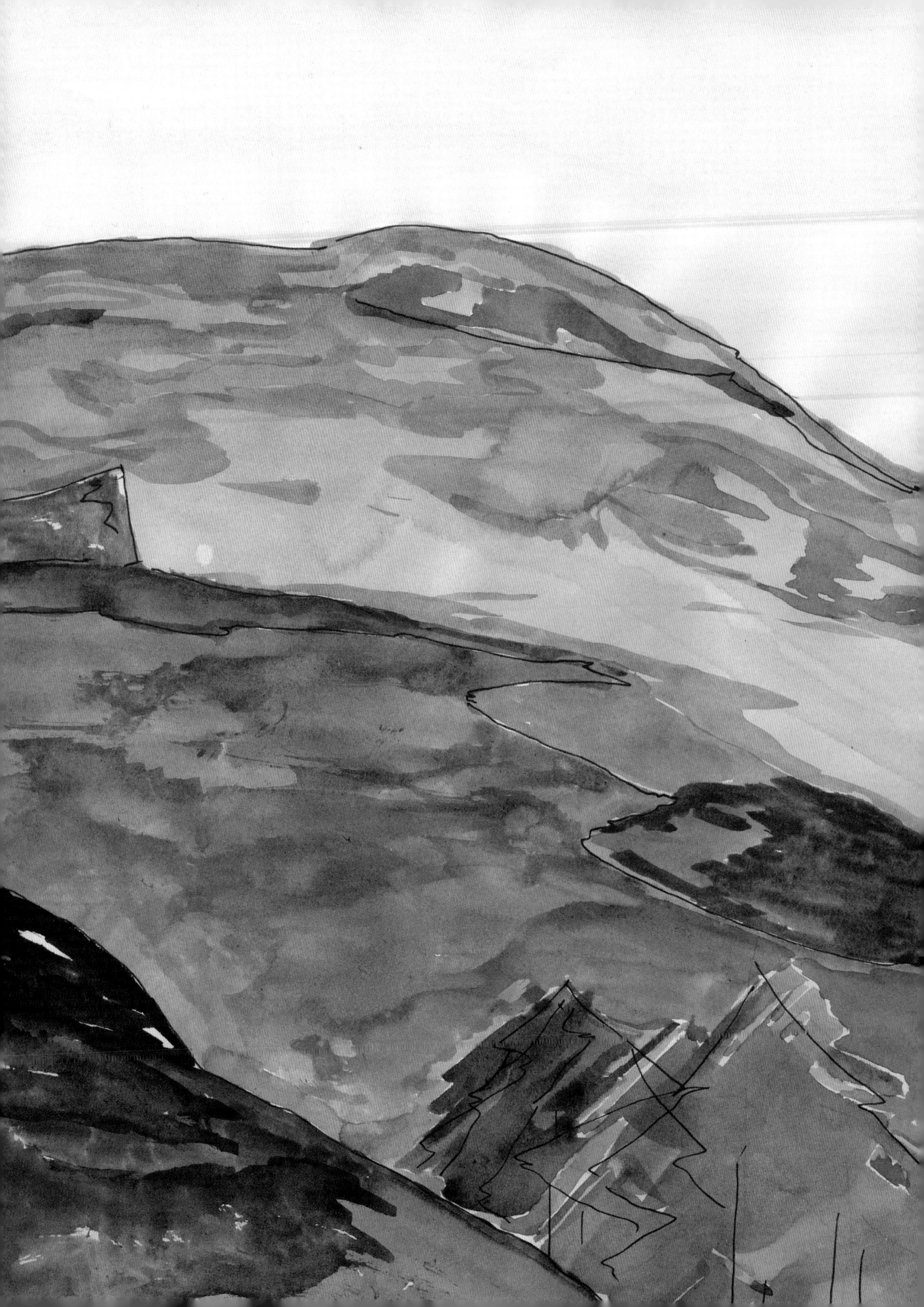

Before too long, on some sunny morning, John would come to take Yellow Boatie back to the waters of Blue Hill Bay. They would have another summer of work and adventure.

THE END

This book is dedicated in loving memory to Gina and Cori Gray.

Acknowledgements

Thanks to my great-grandson Chris Gray, for his one-of-a-kind illustrations in this book, and to my family and friends. Special thanks to Annette and John Candage. With the publication of this book by WoodenBoat Books, Yellow Boatie has found a home.

Author Helen Sylvester was born in Maine in 1919, and has lived in the same house overlooking Blue Hill Bay for nearly seventy years. Fifty three of those years were shared with her late husband, John, a third-generation Mainer.

Illustrator Chris Gray was also born in Maine, and was raised on the Blue Hill Peninsula. He studied at the Maine College of Art, in Portland, Maine, and received his degree in furniture and cabinet making from the North Bennett Street School, in Boston. He makes his living building custom furniture and cabinetry. You can see his work online at: www.chrisgrayfurniture.com.